The Sloth That Saved Easter

Catherine Adams

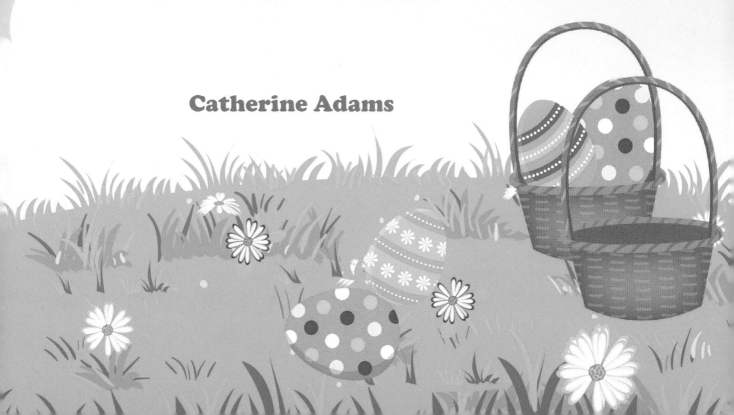

It was the day before Easter and the Easter bunny was busy, busy, busy!

But when the Easter Bunny tried to do everything at once, she slipped and.....WHOOOA....everything flew everywhere and the Easter Bunny landed with a THUD.

"Oh No! I broke my paw!" cried the Easter Bunny. "I won't be able to decorate or hide the eggs. I won't be able to fill or deliver the baskets! I am going to need help with Easter this year!"

So the Easter Bunny put out a sign.
Word spread fast that the Easter Bunny needed
help and soon....

HELP WANTED!!!
- decorating eggs
- hiding eggs
- **filling baskets**
- delivering baskets

Fox quietly raced in to help.

HELP WANTED!!!
- decorating eggs
- hiding eggs
- **filling baskets**
- delivering baskets

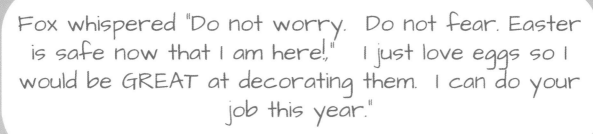

Fox whispered "Do not worry. Do not fear. Easter is safe now that I am here!," I just love eggs so I would be GREAT at decorating them. I can do your job this year."

So fox dashed off to paint eggs.

"Sorry, Easter Bunny, I guess I love eggs a little too much." said Fox.

"Oh no!" cried the Easter Bunny, "that won't do at all!"

Next Squirrel ran to help!

HELP WANTED!!!
- decorating eggs
- hiding eggs
- filling baskets
- delivering baskets

"Do not worry. Do not fear. Easter is safe now that I am here!" squeaked Squirrel. "I am GREAT at hiding things! I can do your job this year!"

So squirrel scampered off to hide some eggs.

Squirrel was back in a flash! "I hid the eggs in my favorite spots so no one will ever find them!" said Squirrel.

Then Kangaroo hopped in to help.

HELP WANTED!!!
- decorating eggs
- hiding eggs
- filling baskets
- delivering baskets

"Do not worry. Do not fear
Easter is safe now that I am here!" said
Kangaroo. "I am GREAT at hopping! Let me
show you how fast I can fill baskets!"

"Sorry, Easter Bunny," said Kangaroo, "but Baby Kangaroo loves chocolate."

"Oh no!" cried the Easter Bunny, "that won't do at all!"

Next Monkey swung in to help.

HELP WANTED!!!
 — decorating eggs
  — hiding eggs
 — filling baskets
 — delivering baskets

But soon Monkey and the baskets were flying everywhere!

"Oh no! That won't do at all!" sobbed the Easter Bunny. "I am just going to have to cancel Easter this year!"

HELP WANTED!!!
– decorating eggs
– hiding eggs
– filling baskets
– delivering baskets

The Easter Bunny didn't notice that someone else had come to help.

The other animals chuckled. They laughed. They rolled their eyes. They all cried "Sloth, you are wwaaayy to slow to be the Easter Bunny!"

But the Easter Bunny wanted to know Sloth's idea. "Sloth, how can you help?" asked the Easter Bunny.

"You know what? You might be right! If we work together, we can be done tonight!" said Squirrel and Kangaroo.

So Squirrel painted the eggs,
just as fast as could be.

And Kangaroo hopped around
hiding eggs in no time at all.

And Monkey filled Easter baskets in a jiffy.

And fox quietly delivered the Easter baskets.

"Thank you Sloth!," said the Easter Bunny. "You showed us that we are GREAT in our own way"

"And that if we work together we can do anything" said Sloth. "And now I think it's time for...